Senior Moments

by Frederick Stroppel

A SAMUEL FRENCH ACTING EDITION

SAMUEL FRENCH

FOUNDED 1830

SAMUELFRENCH.COM

MUSIC USE NOTE

IMPORTANT BILLING AND CREDIT REQUIREMENTS

These plays were all developed at The Theatre Artists Workshop of Westport, and first performed at its theater in Norwalk, CT.

AFTER THE BALL, LOUIE'S DAUGHTER and GLACIER BAY were performed together as an evening of one-acts under the title DANGER, PEOPLE AT LARGE at the Quick Center for the Arts at Fairfield University.

TABLE OF CONTENTS

SNEEZE

SNEEZE was first produced was produced by The Theatre Artists Workshop of Westport in Norwalk Ct., in July 2001, as part of their annual Word of the Week Festival. It was directed by Laurie Eliscu, and had the following cast:

ABBY..Dorothy Bryce
MARTHA.................................Muriel Nussbaum

(ABBY and MARTHA sit on a Park Bench.)

ABBY. *(Pointing.)* Is that him? Over there?

MARTHA. No.

ABBY. Are you sure? It looks like him.

MARTHA. Oh, it's nothing like him.

ABBY. Because if that's the squirrel who stole my Yodel yesterday, I've got a little something for him.

MARTHA. It's not him, Abby.

ABBY. *(Reaches into her bag.)* I've got a nice pretty brick here, and I'm going to smash his furry little head into a bloody pasty pulp. Oh yes, you'll be meeting your maker this day, you shifty little vermin.

MARTHA. It's a different squirrel, Abby. Look, he has a limp. You're not going to tell me a crippled squirrel stole your Yodel.

ABBY. *(Grudgingly.)* Well..I'll bet he knows who did. They're all in this together.

(MARTHA feels the urge to sneeze, but she stifles it.)

MARTHA. *(Smothering her sneeze.)* Nnnngh!

ABBY. What was that?

MARTHA. I almost sneezed.

ABBY. *(Appalled.)* You almost sneezed?

MARTHA. Yes. But I managed to hold it in.

ABBY. What in the world is wrong with you? You should never hold in a sneeze.

MARTHA. I always hold in my sneezes. I've been holding in my sneezes for seventy years.

ABBY. I never heard you hold in a sneeze.

MARTHA. That's because I hardly ever sneeze. But when I do sneeze, I always almost-sneeze. It's just the polite thing to do.

ABBY. But don't you know how dangerous that is? You could pop a blood vessel in your head and have a cerebral hemorrhage.

MARTHA. Oh, I don't think that's going to happen.

ABBY. It may have already happened. Does your head feel funny?

MARTHA. Funny, as in ha-ha?

ABBY. No, funny, as in rivulets of blood seeping into your brain and soaking it like a sponge.

MARTHA. My head feels fine. That's just an old wives' tale.

ABBY. Well - I'm an old wife.

MARTHA. You're an old widow.

ABBY. Not necessarily. Joe's body was never found, you know. He might turn up yet. That would be just like him - just when I'm starting to relax.

MARTHA. Well, the way I see it, if God wants to pop my blood vessel, that's His business. I'm certainly not going to start worrying about sneezing now, at my age.

ABBY. There are practical considerations, Martha. Sometimes when you hold in a sneeze, it slips out the other end. Your muscles get distracted, and whoops! And it's no mild little squeaker, either. No, it fires off like a pistol shot. Nothing polite about that.

MARTHA. Que sera, sera. As my sainted mother always said, "wherever you be, let your wind be free."

ABBY. Yes, I shared an elevator with your mother once, and it is an experience I have never quite shaken. *(Spots another squirrel, grabs the brick.)* Is that him?

MARTHA. That's not a him. That's a female squirrel.

ABBY. How do you know?

MARTHA. I know. I can tell the sex of any animal just by looking at it. I can tell the sex of fish. Don't ask me how. It's a gift, and a great burden. *(Stifling another sneeze.)* Nnnngh!

ABBY. Don't do that! You're giving me the willies!

MARTHA. I can't help it. This is how I sneeze. There must be pollen around here somewhere.

ABBY. Your brain is going to blow right out through your ears. And I don't want to sit here and watch. If it weren't for this squirrel I have to kill, I'd leave right now.

MARTHA. Nothing's going to happen to my brain. My brain's been the same for seventy years. That's just an old wives tale. Another thing they say: if you cross your eyes, they'll stay that way. Well, I've been crossing my eyes at parties and social gatherings for seventy years, and they're still straight as a string.

ABBY. That's true. And they say if you eat breadcrusts, you'll get curly hair. I've been eating breadcrusts from here to Timbuktu, and look - *(Points to her hair.)* - Not a curl. I should look like Shirley Temple by now. That was my dream.

MARTHA. It's just a lot of hooey, in my opinion. They also say that if you, excuse the expression, 'masturbate', your palms will grow hair.

ABBY. But that only goes for men.

MARTHA. Yes, because women don't use their palms, as a rule.

ABBY. No. Although I wouldn't be a bit surprised if Alice Farkus used her palms. That woman's got hair growing out of all kinds of God-awful places. And tough little hairs, too. Like hog bristles.

MARTHA. She makes wonderful pies, though.

ABBY. That she does. Anyway, I don't think you could really get hairy palms from doing that.

MARTHA. No, probably not.

ABBY. It's just another old wives' tale.

MARTHA. *(Beat.)* Of course, it does cause blindness.

ABBY. Oh, yes. Many's the time I've passed a blind person and observed, "There, but for the grace of my own incontestable will..."

MARTHA. I feel so sorry for them, the poor pathetic self-abusers.

ABBY. Of course, on the plus side, now that they're blind, they can diddle themselves as much as they want.

MARTHA. But they can't read any dirty books.

ABBY. *(Nods.)* It's a vicious circle.

(Beat.)

MARTHA. Who were the old wives, anyway?

ABBY. What do you mean?

MARTHA. The old wives - was it like a club?

ABBY. A club? You mean like an Old Wives Club?

MARTHA. Yes - do you think all the old wives sat around a table and came up with these tales, or were they just random old wives over the years, and then some bright fellow collected all the tales in a book or something?

ABBY. I really don't know.

MARTHA. Because I've never read it.

ABBY. Neither have I.

MARTHA. And yet we both know so many old wives' tales.

ABBY. Word-of-mouth, I guess.

MARTHA. It's a testament to all the old wives in the world, wherever they may be.

ABBY. I wish that squirrel would come. I have to get home for Judge Judy.

MARTHA. And it makes you wonder - who's going to pass these stories on after we're gone?

ABBY. That's true enough. The old traditions are dying.

MARTHA. People get their information from machines nowadays.

ABBY. Soon we'll all be robots. We won't sneeze or break wind or anything.

MARTHA. It's very sad.

ABBY. *(Excited.)* Here he comes! That's him! And look - he's got a Ring-Ding in his mouth! Bold as brass, that one! *(Takes up the brick.)* Now I've got you, you cocky little weasel. Your chickens have finally come home to roost.

MARTHA. Oh, let him finish the Ring-Ding, Abby. That's the humane thing to do.

ABBY. *(Scoffs.)* I didn't get this far in life by being sentimental. Come on, Mr. Squirrel, just a little closer, just one more step...

(ABBY raises the brick ready to strike. Suddenly...)

MARTHA. AH-CHOOO!

ABBY. Oh no!

MARTHA. *(Proudly.)* Say, did you hear that sneeze?

ABBY. *(Outraged.)* Did I hear it? Did I hear it?

MARTHA. That was a corker, wasn't it?

ABBY. He's gone! You chased him away! I had him right in my sights, he was dead meat, and you spoiled it with your goddamn sneeze! Now he knows me. Now I've lost his trust. I'll never get that close again. Oh, my one chance to kill a living thing, my one chance to give my life purpose and meaning - and you couldn't hold in one lousy sneeze, you selfish, inconsiderate bitch...!

MARTHA. *(Holding her head.)* Ohhh...

ABBY. What's the matter?

MARTHA. My head.

ABBY. What?

MARTHA. It feels funny.

ABBY. *(Apprehensive.)* Funny as in ha-ha?

(MARTHA falls over on the bench. Blackout.)

A WORLD OF PLEASURE

A WORLD OF PLEASURE was first produced by The Theatre Artists Workshop of Westport in Norwalk CT, in October 2004, as part of their annual Playwrights One-Act Festival. It was directed by Mark Graham, and had the following cast:

CUSTOMER...................................Bill Phillips
STANLEY..Herb Duncan
EMILY...Betty Jinnette

(An empty store. STANLEY, an elderly man, is busy packing up a box for shipping. A CUSTOMER, a man in his 30's, enters the shop. He looks around in surprise at the empty shelves.)

CUSTOMER. Hi. Are you open?

STANLEY. No sir. As a matter of fact, we're closing up. Closing up shop.

CUSTOMER. Really?

STANLEY. After thirty-three years. All finished. Last nail in the coffin.

CUSTOMER. Thirty-three years...! Gee, I'm sorry.

STANLEY. *(Shrugs.)* That's the way of the world, young fella. It's all superstores and big chains now. Everything's Disney-fied, you know what I'm saying? No place for the little corner Mom-and-Pop business anymore. And it's a damn shame. The personal touch is gone. Gone.

(EMILY, STANLEY's wife, ENTERS carrying a small oblong box.)

EMILY. Stanley, dear - where are we putting the vibrators?

STANLEY. There's a box over there. This is my wife, Emily.

EMILY. *(Bright smile.)* Hello - welcome to Pleasure World! *(Looks for box.)* I don't see it.

STANLEY. Right there. See where it says "dildos"?

EMILY. But it's not a dildo, dear. It's a vibrator.

STANLEY. *(Dismissive.)* Oh, same thing.

EMILY. It's not the same thing. A dildo is not a vibrator. *(To CUSTOMER.)* We've been having this argument for the last thirty years.

STANLEY. Thirty-three. *(To CUSTOMER.)* What do you say? Same family, right?

CUSTOMER. But a vibrator has batteries, yes...?

EMILY. Exactly. It's battery-operated, it has moving parts. Thank you.

STANLEY. *(Shrugs.)* I'm always wrong.

EMILY. Like saying a flashlight is the same as a candle...!

(She heads into the back.)

STANLEY. All right, calm down, don't get a bee in your bonnet. *(After she EXITS.)* She's a caution, isn't she? But good-hearted. I should introduce myself: Stanley Pleasure.

CUSTOMER. *(As they shake hands.)* Pleasure? That's your last name?

STANLEY. *(Nods.)* I changed it. Figured it would be good for business.

CUSTOMER. So you started this store, you and your wife?

STANLEY. 1971. Back during that whole Sexual Revolution thing. Yep, built those shelves myself, painted the signs, hung the curtains on the peep-show booths. A real labor of love. Oh, we had some good times here. If these walls could talk...

CUSTOMER. What happened? Business fell off?

STANLEY. *(Nods.)* City's been trying to close us down for years anyway. We don't fit the "neighborhood profile". Guess that means we're too working class. Damn rich yuppies, they order their sex toys on the internet now, they think they don't need us. They'll find out. *(Brightly.)* But enough of my bellyaching. What can I do for you, sir?

CUSTOMER. Oh, I don't want to bother you, you're busy here...

STANLEY. Nonsense. We never let a customer leave unsatisfied. What do you need? Condoms? We got all kinds of condoms. Neon, rainbow-colored.. I think they're in this box here. *(Checks box.)* No, those are cock-rings. *(Browsing.)* And nipple clamps... Don't suppose you have any use for nipple clamps?

CUSTOMER. Actually - I was looking for an inflatable doll.

STANLEY. Inflatable doll?

CUSTOMER. It's for a bachelor party.

STANLEY. 'Course it is. Why else would you want one? *(Looks around.)* I'm just not sure if they're out here... *(Calls out.)* Emily!

EMILY. Yes?

STANLEY. Blow-up dolls?

EMILY. *(Emerging from the backroom.)* With or without the functional hoo-ha?

CUSTOMER. Uh...

STANLEY. With, right? If you're gonna spend the money, that's the way to go.

EMILY. It's self-lubricating.

CUSTOMER. Oh, Well, sure.

EMILY. Blonde, redhead...?

CUSTOMER. Doesn't matter. *(On second thought.)* Redhead.

(EMILY EXITS into the back room.)

STANLEY. I do hear that some folks put them in the front seat of their car, so's they can use the HOV lane. And. of course, there's Halloween. It's a versatile item, you definitely get your money's worth. *(Beat.)* She'll be just a second. I'd offer you something to eat, but we already disconnected the hot plate and the Mr. Coffee. Oh, I know - *(Reaches into a box, takes out a package.)* Edible panties. Very tasty, I'm told.

CUSTOMER. I'm not really hungry.

STANLEY. *(Looks at labels.)* These are cherry, and these are peppermint.

CUSTOMER. *(Shrugs.)* Cherry.

STANLEY. Cherry it is. And here's some chocolate body paint. Do a little rip and dip, you've got yourself a meal.

CUSTOMER. Thanks. *(As they snack.)* Mmm. So, a lot of history in this place, I'll bet. Any celebrities ever stop in?

STANLEY. Oh, you betcha. Personal appearances, photo ops and such. Where's that box with the pictures...? Here. (Goes to a box, takes out a framed photo.) Look, here we are with Al Goldstein. The editor of Screw? He was a pioneer of the industry. We all owe him a great debt. *(Finds other 8 X 10s.)* And here's Marilyn Chambers... Annie Sprinkle...

CUSTOMER. *(Reads inscription.)* "Thanks for last night, Big Boy."

STANLEY. She was only joshing. It still gets Emily's goat, though. *(More photos.)* Long John Holmes...Linda Lovelace; what a sweetheart...

CUSTOMER. *(Re:photo.)* Who's this?

STANLEY. That's Donna Matrix. She's one of those S and M gals. Used to buy all her whips from us. Ten at a time, she went through them so fast. Well, look at the arms on her. Big-boned. But a warm and personable lady. And a heck of a cook. She used to invite us over to her apartment for dinner - she would make her special goulash? - and swear to God, she always had some guy tied to a chair or trussed up from the chandelier. Never a dull moment.

CUSTOMER. *(Intrigued by photo.)* So she lives nearby?

STANLEY. No, not anymore. Professional mishap. Seems she was riding this fellow like a horse, swinging her riding crop and such, and I guess she must have flicked him on his private parts or whatever, but something spooked him, he reared up and threw her. And she hit her head on a radiator, scrambled her brains but good. She's out East now, in some home, doesn't know who she is. So you see, we should count ourselves lucky - at least we've got our memories.

(EMILY returns with a blow-up doll in a package.)

EMILY. Here you go. The Rita Hayworth Deluxe. Comes with its own little air pump. *(Notices STANLEY snacking.)* What are you eating? You're not supposed to be snacking, with your sugar count.

STANLEY. Oh, it's a special occasion, Mother.

EMILY. Won't be so special when they cart you off to the hospital. Come on, give it here. *(Sees photos lying around.)* And what's all this junk lying around? You're supposed to be packing. Honestly.

STANLEY. I was showing him some memorabilia. Remember Al Goldstein?

EMILY. Ugh. He was all hands, that man.

STANLEY. Tell me about it. *(Shows another photo, grins.)* Hey, Annie Sprinkle...

EMILY. *(Annoyed.)* I still say you wrote that yourself. *(She holds up a movie reel.)* Speaking of memorabilia, look what I found in the back.

STANLEY. Hey, look at that! One of the old films. My my! *(To CUSTOMER.)* Back in the early days, we had a little theater in the back, regular patrons only, it was just a screen and a projector, and we'd have our own Film Festivals, Russ Meyer marathons, so forth... *(About reel.)* Which one is this?

EMILY. The Naughty Cheerleaders.

STANLEY. *(Fondly.)* Our first Triple-X!

EMILY. We watched it together, remember?

STANLEY. Do I ever. Made some popcorn, and you had your pompoms from high school... *(They have a moment of glowing remembrance.)* Folks nowadays don't know what they're missing. Seeing it up on there on the big screen...! Of course they have these fancy DVDs now, you can skip from one scene to the next, cut right to the highlights. Which is convenient, if you're pressed for time.

EMILY. *(Disapproving.)* But that's no way to watch a movie. For instance, The Naughty Cheerleaders: if you don't watch the beginning, when Pamela arrives off the bus and wins the big audition with a dramatic double-somersault-into-a-split, you miss the whole point of the gang-bang.

STANLEY. True, but I still think that sequence stands by itself.

EMILY. You like action all the time. I prefer a story with characters.

STANLEY. All right, Mother, enough with the shop talk. We're boring this young man. He wants to get home with his parcel.

CUSTOMER. No, I find this all very interesting. You know, I go into sex shops all the time...

STANLEY. *(Corrects him.)* Adult boutiques, please.

CUSTOMER. Of course - and all I see are the porno magazines and the leather paddles. It's nice to put a human face to it all.

STANLEY. We're just a simple hard-working couple, hounded and persecuted by the puritanical Furies of corporate America.

CUSTOMER. Well, that's a disgrace, it really is. They should be giving you landmark status or something. Or a medal! All the aid and succor you've given to lonely frustrated people all over this great city... And what are they putting here instead? Another Starbucks, I suppose?

EMILY. *(Hopeful.)* Maybe a Krispy Kreme.

STANLEY. Some people call that progress.

CUSTOMER. And what's going to happen to you? You dedicate your life to a calling, where do you go from here?

STANLEY. Don't worry about us. We'll be heading upstate after we close, got a nice piece of property in Putnam County.

EMILY. Stanley thinks he's going to raise sheep.

STANLEY. Always been a dream of mine. Those curly little heads...! And my cousin runs a strip club over in New Paltz, so I'll be serving there in an advisory capacity. Keeping my hand in, so to speak. *(Sighs.)* Still, we're gonna miss this place.

EMILY. Don't start.

STANLEY. I never thought we'd close. All those years...

EMILY. *(Starts to cry.)*

STANLEY. *(Comforting her.)* All right, Mother. It's all right.

(CUSTOMER watches the tender scene, makes up his mind.)

CUSTOMER. You know, maybe there's something I can do.

STANLEY. There is, son, there is. You take your doll home, have a corking good time with it, and may your life be always happy and sexually bountiful.

EMILY. *(Looks up, sniffling.)* That's a lovely thought, dear.

CUSTOMER. Seriously. I know some people in real estate who are familiar with this area. Maybe we could locate an alternate venue where you could set up shop.

STANLEY. You mean, move the business somewhere else?

CUSTOMER. Exactly.

EMILY. Oh, I don't think we want to start all over again. We're not young anymore, appearances to the contrary.

CUSTOMER. You won't be starting over. You have an inventory, you have a brand name. *(Indicates photos.)* You have testimonials.

STANLEY. But all that rigmarole, with the leases and the licenses...

CUSTOMER. I'm in merchandising, I can help you with all that. Stanley, Emily - I want to be a part of this.

EMILY. We appreciate your support, but we've sorta got our hearts set on that farm.

STANLEY. And the sheep.

CUSTOMER. You'll excuse me for saying so, but this goes way beyond personal considerations. A place like this - there's a whole world of memories and historic associations contained within these four walls, and it has to be preserved, for the sake of future generations. Gee, when I was a kid, thirteen or so, I remember sneaking into an adult store just like this one, maybe even a little rattier, and looking at all the wild, magical gadgets, and the glossy magazines, and the videos under the glass cases, titles like "Leave it to Beavers", "Back-Door Babes" - "The Erotic Adventures of Pinocchio" - and everywhere you looked, everywhere, pictures of naked women, thousands of them, kneeling, squatting, riding ponies - God, it was Wonderland! My head was exploding! I walked out - well, I was thrown out - on an emotional high. Just knowing that this secret garden existed, and that someday, somehow, I would be back to drink from its intoxicating spring - ! That's a promise and a joy that today's teenagers will never know. They push a computer button, and it's right there in their homes, cheap and unearned - all the mystery, all the drama, gone! It's like when they got rid of the Latin Mass, you know? And maybe it's inevitable, but should we just sit back and let it happen? Should we let another seminal tradition perish without protest? Or should we take a stand right here, right now, against the yahoos of modern culture, and say "Enough! Not on my watch! No fucking way!" You'll pardon my French.

STANLEY. *(Moved by his peroration.)* Dammit, you're right. We did contribute to making the world a happier place, we did provide relief to our fellow men - why should we be tossed aside like garbage?

EMILY. Because that's life, dear. That's the way it goes.

STANLEY. But it doesn't have to go, Emily!

CUSTOMER. No, by God, it doesn't. You can't let all this die.

STANLEY. Who are these know-nothings to tell me when and where I can ply my trade? I've forgotten more about pornography than most of those young cyber-punks will ever know.

CUSTOMER. You're a national resource, and you shouldn't go untapped.

STANLEY. There's still plenty of gas left in the old tank. *(Getting excited.)* You know, I've always wanted to have a really first-rate adult boutique, with neon signs for all the different sections, and video monitors, and an ATM machine.

EMILY. *(Getting into the spirit.)* Maybe the customers could have a credit card, for special discounts, one of those little doodads you put right on your key ring...?

STANLEY. And a cafe off to the side, like they have at that Barnes and Nobles place - folks can sit, browse, have coffee -

EMILY. Krispy Kremes!

STANLEY. Little erotic cannolis... It could be a regular meeting place. An event in itself.

EMILY. I always thought a gift-wrap section would be nice. And maybe I could run a craft booth. *(To CUSTOMER.)* You know, a lot of these things are so expensive, and you can really make them yourself.

STANLEY. And a play area for the kids, with the video games....and an indoor carousel... Internet access... Nude ping-pong...! *(Clutches his heart.)* Ohhh! Uh-Oh...

(He staggers to the side.)

CUSTOMER. *(Catches his arm.)* Stanley! Are you all right?

STANLEY. *(Murmuring weakly.)* Ping-pong...ping-pong...

EMILY. I knew this would happen. All that sugar. *(EMILY clears packing material off a chair, helps STANLEY sit down.)* Here we go...

CUSTOMER. Is there anything we should do?

EMILY. I have his pills right here.

(Fishes a vial of pills from her bag.)

STANLEY. *(Mumbling.)* Buy one, get one free...all sales final....

EMILY. Here you go, Stanley. Open your mouth.

STANLEY. *(Mumbles.)* No thanks, I'm just looking.

EMILY. Under your tongue. *(She pops a pill into his mouth.)* There. He'll be fine now. He gets over-stimulated. It's an occupational hazard.

CUSTOMER. I'm sorry, I had no idea...

EMILY. He has the heart of a Viking, but the arteries are a different story altogether. *(As STANLEY revives.)* Are you all right, dear?

STANLEY. What am I sitting on?

(Stanley reaches beneath him, pulls out a long rubber phallus.)

EMILY. Well, we know what box that goes in.

(EMILY puts the item in the Dildo box.)

STANLEY. *(To CUSTOMER, sheepish.)* Sorry about that. Went a little out-of-focus there.

CUSTOMER. No, it's my fault. I've taken up enough of your time, you need your rest. *(About the doll.)* Let me just pay for this, and I'll get out of your way. How much...?

EMILY. Oh, take it.

CUSTOMER. Just take it?

EMILY. With our blessings.

STANLEY. In fact, take everything, why don't you?

CUSTOMER. Pardon?

STANLEY. *(Rising from his chair.)* The whole works. Go off and find that prime location you were talking about, and start a business of your own.

CUSTOMER. But I don't know anything about the adult industry.

STANLEY. You'll pick it up as you go along. The most important thing is the desire, and you've got that in spades. Oh, no question - I see a little of myself in you. The same fire in the belly, the same eye of the tiger. You'll do just fine.

CUSTOMER. But what about you, Stanley?

STANLEY. *(Smiles at EMILY.)* We've had our run. Time to pass the baton. Sure, take it all, the movies, the lotions, the dildos and the vibrators. *(Beat.)* I'd just like to keep a few souvenirs. You don't mind, Mother, do you?

EMILY. Of course not. Thirty years worth of memories.

STANLEY. Thirty-three. *(Holds up photo.)* Couldn't give up Annie.

EMILY. Old fool.

CUSTOMER. *(Thoughtful.)* Gee, maybe I could do it. Why not? I just have to give my notice at WalMart...But the opportunity is ripe, the market is there. Someone has to take up the reins - why not me? The only thing is - well, I know this is a lot to ask, but I don't suppose you'd let me call it Pleasure World?

(STANLEY and EMILY share a look.)

STANLEY. *(Breaks into a smile.)* We'd be honored.

(They shake hands. The CUSTOMER starts out, excited.)

STANLEY. Enjoy your bachelor party.
CUSTOMER. What bachelor party—? *(STANLEY points to inflat-able doll.)* Oh - right.

(CUSTOMER EXITS.)

STANLEY. Nice young fellow. *(Impressed.)* WalMart.
EMILY. And you go filling his head with crazy dreams.
STANLEY. We're in the dream business, Emily.
EMILY. *(Sighs.)* Oh, Stanley, I'm going to miss this place, I really am.

(STANLEY picks up the Cheerleaders reel.)

STANLEY. What do you say? For old times sake?

(EMILY thinks it over.)

EMILY. I'll get the pom-poms.
STANLEY. *(Picks up edible panties and chocolate sauce.)* I've got the snacks.

(He follows her off.)

AFTER THE BALL

AFTER THE BALL was produced by The Theatre Artists Workshop of Westport in Norwalk CT, in October 2003, as part of their annual Playwrights One-Act Festival. It was directed by Brett Somers, and had the following cast:

STEWART.................................Chilton Ryan
JOANNA.......................................Nadine Willig

AFTER THE BALL was part of an evening of one-acts titled DANGER, PEOPLE AT LARGE, at the Quick Center for the Arts at Fairfield University in Fairfield, CT, in April 2005. It was produced by Tom Zingarelli and directed by Doug Moser with the follwoing cast and production staff:

STEWART.................................Jack Klugman
JOANNA.......................................Brett Somers

Set Designer: Mark Cheney
Lighting Designer: Nicole Dessin
Sound Designer: Chris Swetcky
Soundboard Operator: Joe Boerst
Lightboard Operator: Zina Skachinksy
Technical Director: Russ Nagy
Stage Manager: Theresa Stark

(STEWART and JOANNA, a well-dressed middle-aged couple, ENTER their house. JOANNA carries a table centerpiece. STEWART is wearing a flowered lei. HE falls into a chair, exhausted.)

STEWART. God, that was a good funeral. I was sorry to see it end.

JOANNA. And you thought you were going to have such a bad time.

STEWART. I know.

JOANNA. Had to practically drag you.

STEWART. *(Unties his shoes.)* Well, I'm not too big on funerals as a rule, but I'm glad I went. It was a complete delight.

JOANNA. Want something to drink?

STEWART. Maybe coffee, that's all.

JOANNA. I'll put on a pot.

(JOANNA EXITS into kitchen.)

STEWART. *(Rubs his feet.)* No, it started right at the church, with the balloons, and just took off from there. Never a dull moment. But that's Charlie for you. An entertainer, right to the end.

JOANNA. *(From offstage.)* Yes, he definitely set the tone.

STEWART. Being buried in a clown suit...! *(Shakes head, laughs.)* How did they manage to close the casket over those big shoes?

(JOANNA returns with her drink.)

JOANNA. They were collapsible. Like an accordion.

STEWART. They didn't leave that red nose on him when they buried him, did they?

JOANNA. I wouldn't be surprised.

STEWART. Imagine if they had to dig him up, a hundred years from now? My, my. *(Chuckles at the thought.)* And they had some kind of speaker rigged inside the coffin. It sounded like he was snoring. How

27

did he come up with all those ridiculous ideas?

JOANNA. He had plenty of time.

STEWART. That's true.

JOANNA. The pallbearers were cute.

STEWART. I was surprised - I thought Rockettes had to be taller than that.

JOANNA. It's a stage illusion. Did you see them kicking? *(She kicks her leg in modest imitation.)* "It's not where you start, it's where you finish..."

STEWART. And the confetti, the streamers...

JOANNA. Quite a production.

STEWART. First-rate. You know, you go to some funerals, and you can tell they were just pulled together at the last minute. This was carefully thought out. Programs in the pews, valet parking... the calliope at the cemetery. All those little grace notes. Nothing left to chance.

JOANNA. And then the party.

STEWART. Well, the party was something else again. Incredible.

JOANNA. He wanted to rent out the Huntington Town House, but obviously he couldn't give them a definite date.

STEWART. But the backyard was fine, with the big tent. I'll bet that cost a pretty penny.

JOANNA. Ten thousand dollars, and that's without the food.

STEWART. The food! I thought we were just going to have cold cuts and potato salad. Or a six-foot hero. But Lobster Newburg, rack of lamb...! What was that dessert I had? With the cream and the...

JOANNA. Trifle.

STEWART. Trifle, yes! Delicious. Look, I got some on my tie.

JOANNA. And on your sleeve, too.

STEWART. I couldn't stop eating. And I was full from the cocktail hour. The fried octopus. The caviar...!

JOANNA. Oh! And the coconut shrimp...!

STEWART. Well - I don't get that whole coconut shrimp thing.

JOANNA. You won't even try it.

STEWART. How do shrimp and coconut go together? You tell me. Am I supposed to just accept this on faith?

JOANNA. But I think the coconut was a thematic choice - because he was part-Hawaiian.

STEWART. Charlie? Since when?

JOANNA. His grandmother. You knew that.

STEWART. I thought she was from Guam.

SENIOR MOMENTS

JOANNA. Guam, Hawaii... the Pacific Rim. That's why the leis.

STEWART. These are real flowers, you know. Must have cost a fortune.

JOANNA. Charlie wasn't tight. Look at the band - ten pieces, and a singer.

STEWART. They were terrific. I always say, the music makes the party. Had you shaking your whatzis like a hooch dancer.

JOANNA. Oh, you were dancing, too.

STEWART. Not on a table.

JOANNA. Who was leading the conga line?

STEWART. That was... I was heading for the bar, and Denise grabbed me.

JOANNA. She grabbed you, all right. I think she's already lining up her next husband.

STEWART. Oh, stop.

JOANNA. She was a little too happy for a first-time widow, if you ask me.

STEWART. She's been through a rough time. She deserves to blow off some steam.

JOANNA. I should have such a rough time when it's your turn. Charlie's last months were a joy. He never lost his sense of humor, his spirit, no matter how sick he was. It was a real pleasure to visit him in the hospital. He would cheer me up. That's how he lived his whole life. That's even how he died, you know. Died laughing.

STEWART. Not literally?

JOANNA. *(Nods.)* His cousin Peggy told me. He was sitting up in bed, telling one of his jokes, and he started laughing, even before he got to the punchline, and the next thing you know - gone. With a big wide smile on his face.

STEWART. Must have been a hell of a joke.

JOANNA. We'll never know.

STEWART. Well, he would have enjoyed himself today. Every time someone sat down on one of those whoopee cushions - there must have been a hundred of them hidden around the house.

JOANNA. His own version of a 21-gun salute.

STEWART. All in all, quite a day. Just about the perfect party.

JOANNA. Perfect would have been if we'd won the 50-50 Raffle.

STEWART. Don't complain - you got the centerpiece. *(Sighs.)* Yes, today was a revelation to me. Really turned my thinking around. Enough with these grim, somber funerals. All that mourning and grieving - ridiculous, when you think about it. No, so much better to go out in style. Like the Pharoahs.

JOANNA. The who?

STEWART. The Pharoahs, the Romans... all those pagans, they knew how to make an exit. Orgies and fireworks. No dirges or sad songs. If I go to one more funeral where they sing "Candle in the Wind"...! It should be a celebration, dammit. You made it to the end of your life, the aggravation is over, so let's party. That's the ticket. That's how I want to die. With a funeral just like that. Lots of laughs, lots of good feeling.

JOANNA. Yes, well - that's not going to happen, God knows.

STEWART. What do you mean?

JOANNA. I mean... well, it won't be a party, that's all.

STEWART. Why not?

JOANNA. Oh, come on, Stewart. What a question. *(STEWART is still waiting.)* It's not you.

STEWART. Not me?

JOANNA. You're not... - oh, how did we get on to this? It's too late. *(Heads off to bed.)* I'm going to turn in. Your coffee's probably ready.

STEWART. Wait a minute. What are you saying here? That I'm not capable of having a happy funeral?

JOANNA. I'm saying - yes, that's what I'm saying.

STEWART. How can you make a statement like that?

JOANNA. Don't take it personally - it's just the way things are. Charlie is one type of person, you're another type. People think of you in a certain way.

STEWART. And what way is that?

JOANNA. Sober. Industrious. Predictable.

STEWART. Predictable? I'm predictable? Why, that's -

JOANNA. *(Anticipates him.)* Ridiculous?

STEWART. Yes! *(Belatedly realizes that he's just been predictable.)* Granted, I have a responsible job at the bank, I have a measure of dignity necessary to secure my position in the community. But I have my zany side, too.

JOANNA. Zany?

STEWART. Yes. Zany. Whimsical. I can cut loose with the best of them.

JOANNA. You've been cutting loose for the past five hours, and look at you - you're still wearing your tie. Even with trifle on it. What does that say?

STEWART. I like this tie. What, it bothers you? *(Pulls off his tie.)* Is that better? See, I can be blithe about my accessories.

JOANNA. You're missing the point, Stewart. The tie is you. You are the tie. Even without the tie, you're still wearing the tie.

STEWART. *(Confused.)* I guess I am missing the point.

JOANNA. It's a matter of personality. You could have the exact same funeral as Charlie - balloons, ice sculptures, cotton candy - it wouldn't work. No one would get it. Because the problem is, you're just not -

(She hesitates.)

STEWART. I'm not what? Why don't you just come out and say it? I'm not what?

JOANNA. You're not funny.

STEWART. What?

JOANNA. You're not funny.

(Beat.)

STEWART. I am so funny.

JOANNA. No, you're not. You're really not. *(STEWART stares at her in disbelief.)* I'm just being honest, dear. You're not funny.

STEWART. That's not true. I'm very funny. I'm just as funny as Charlie. I'm more subtle. I'm droll. *(JOANNA rolls her eyes.)* What about my Indian accent? You always laugh at that. *(A lame Indian accent.)* "Would you like a doughnut with your Slurpee?" *(She doesn't laugh.)* Don't try to hold it in. You know that's funny!

JOANNA. What can I say?

STEWART. You know, this is so typical - I have myself a good day, and you go and spoil it with some mean undermining remark. You have a wide streak of malice in you, Joanna, and it grows more and more unbecoming with age.

JOANNA. All right, I take it back. You're very funny. You're a hoot. You're going to have a marvelous funeral. I can't wait.

STEWART. This is because I wouldn't eat the coconut shrimp? Is that it?

JOANNA. Look, it's very simple: some people are funny; some people are not. You are not.

STEWART. I am funny! I've been funny all my life. Even when I was a kid - at the dinner table, I was always the cut-up. Had my parents in stitches. You can't say I'm not funny. You can't!

JOANNA. Stewart, I don't know if you're repressing your natural humor, or if you lost it in the war. But I've been living with you for twenty-four years, and you're not funny. You're not even close.

STEWART. Really? Well, look at this. *(Takes whoopee cushion from pocket.)* That's right. I took mine with me. And you know what?

(STEWART blows up the whoopee cushion, puts it on a chair, and sits on it. After the fart noise, STEWART waits expectantly)

JOANNA. *(Shrugs.)* Not funny. *(STEWART is upset.)* You can't do anything about it. It's beyond you.

STEWART. I suppose you think you're funny? I suppose you think people are going to have fun at your funeral?

JOANNA. I think they'll walk away with a positive attitude. I know how to enjoy life.

STEWART. We're all well aware of that, aren't we?

JOANNA. Stewart, don't start.

STEWART. I saw you and the mortician - do you think I'm blind? That little business with the Mass cards...?

JOANNA. Hey, I'm a flirt - I've never denied it. Half the men who come to my funeral will think they might have had a shot at me, and what's wrong with that? See, that's my point. Charlie gave everyone something to remember today, and that's what people need. Memories. Hope. There's no hope in your soul, Stewart. There's no joy. People are going to be depressed at your funeral. You have to accept this.

STEWART. *(Can't believe it.)* No one thinks I'm funny? No one?

JOANNA. I'm not saying that you're rampantly, overbearingly un-funny. Nobody recoils at your approach; almost everyone has a genuine fondness for you, I think. But you don't exactly brighten up a room when you walk in. You don't give people a reason for living.

STEWART. Not the way Charlie did.

JOANNA. Charlie had a gift. His smile was a sunburst. Yours is a pale, mirthless clench. It connotes pain.

STEWART. So what you're saying is, you really would have pre-ferred Charlie to me.

JOANNA. I didn't say that.

STEWART. But would you have? The man's dead now, you can tell me.

JOANNA. *(Evasive.)* I don't think this is a profitable area for specu-lation...

STEWART. Aha! So you would!

JOANNA. Well, who wouldn't, for God's sake? Charlie was charming and frisky right to his last breath. Even now, six feet under, he's got more life in him than you do.

STEWART. That's fine. In a choice between me and a corpse...

JOANNA. You're making it very hard for me to be diplomatic.

STEWART. If you thought Charlie was such a ball of fire, why didn't you hook up with him while he was alive? *(Sharply.)* Or did you?

JOANNA. All I did was suggest that you're not the most high-spirited person in the world, and right away you accuse me of being unfaithful. My God, if we can't be honest with each other...!

STEWART. I'll be honest with you. I think you had an affair with Charlie Pemberton!

JOANNA. Go get your coffee, will you? You're making a fool of yourself.

STEWART. I think you besmirched our marriage vows with a vulgar attention-grabbing semi-Polynesian buffoon who had himself buried in a clown suit!

JOANNA. Don't lash out at me because you can't deal with your own unfunniness!

STEWART. *(Furious.)* I AM FUNNY! I AM! *(Beat, as he composes himself.)* And I'll tell you something else: Denise thinks I'm funny.

JOANNA. Oh, she does?

STEWART. She thinks my Indian accent is hilarious. Hilarious. Gets a big kick out of it. And guess who she doesn't think is funny? You!

JOANNA. Oh, please. Of course I'm funny.

STEWART. *(Taunting.)* No, you're not. No, you're not.

JOANNA. Stewart - look.

(JOANNA makes a funny face. STEWART tries not to smile, but he can't help it, and bursts out laughing.)

STEWART. It's only because I'm an easy audience.

JOANNA. Not as easy as Denise, it appears. And I'd like to know, when did she have occasion to hear your corny Seven-Eleven routine?

STEWART. Ah, wouldn't you like to know?

JOANNA. *(Laughs.)* Now that's funny. You and Denise...! Although, I have to admit, you two would be perfect for each other. There's a woman who never had an original or interesting thought in her life.

STEWART. Oh, I see how this works - everyone's boring, except you and Charlie. You have something special, with your clever banter and your big stupid smiles. Well, let's face it, Denise must have had some kind of sense of humor, to go through with this ridiculous funeral - yes, ridiculous - throwing all that good money away to indulge some pathetic egomaniacal fantasy...!

JOANNA. Denise had nothing to do with it. If it had been up to her...

(JOANNA catches herself. Beat, as the dawn breaks for STEWART.)

STEWART. You planned the funeral, didn't you?

JOANNA. Me? Don't be silly.

STEWART. Of course. You knew about the collapsible shoes. And the cost of the tent...

JOANNA. His cousin Peggy told me...

STEWART. His cousin Peggy had her nose in a pitcher of beer from the minute we got there. No, it all makes sense now. I remember, you made me stop outside the church to watch the altar boys break-dance. You knew that was going to happen. Because you were running the whole operation.

JOANNA. Everything was Charlie's idea.

STEWART. You said yourself, he couldn't have arranged everything before he died. Somebody had to order the balloons, and the Rockettes, and the coconut shrimp! Face it, Joanna, your fingerprints are all over this sordid charade. That's why you were running up to the hospital every day with your organizer and your freshly-sharpened pencils. I can see you now, in bed together, sketching out ideas, brainstorming, and laughing, laughing...!

JOANNA. No!

STEWART. Yes, yes! Perhaps you were even trading quips and working up a fine comic froth the day he seized up and died!

JOANNA. That's a lie!

STEWART. You put that big sunburst on his face, didn't you? Didn't you?

(JOANNA slaps STEWART's face. After a stunned moment, STEWART smiles bitterly.)

STEWART. I'm smiling to connote pain. *(JOANNA turns away, mortified.)* I don't know what's a worse betrayal - letting me think I was funny all these years when I wasn't, or sneaking behind my back to plan another man's funeral.

JOANNA. Stewart - it was a creative challenge for me. It had no personal meaning.

STEWART. I wish I could believe that. But I have no illusions now. To think, you were faking all those laughs...!

JOANNA. Not all, Stewart. Not all!

(Beat.)

STEWART. I'm going to get my coffee.

JOANNA. Stewart...!

STEWART. *(Quietly.)* I don't want a happy funeral. I want it to be lugubrious and unpleasant, and completely predictable. I don't want anyone to be left with a fond memory of me. As my wife, will you see to it?

JOANNA. Of course - if that's what you want.

STEWART. That's what I want.

JOANNA. *(Beat.)* Stewart, can you ever forgive me?

STEWART. Forgive you? I'm grateful, Joanna. You've let me see myself clear for the first time. I'm an unfunny man. That's who I am.

(STEWART turns to EXIT.)

JOANNA. Wait, please! *(HE stops.)* I have something for you. *(JOANNA goes to her pocketbook. She fishes out a red clown nose. She hands it to STEWART, who takes it gingerly.)* It was Charlie's.

STEWART. You took it right off his cold nose?

JOANNA. Yes. And now I want you to have it.

STEWART. *(Handing it back.)* No, I couldn't...

JOANNA. Charlie would have wanted someone to carry on for him. I know you can do it.

(STEWART looks pensively at the red nose.)

STEWART. There's still some clown make-up on it.

JOANNA. Put it on. Please.

(STEWART slowly puts the red nose on. He waits for a reaction.)

JOANNA. *(Smiles.)* You look...funny.

(STEWART is touched.)

STEWART. *(With quiet emotion.)* Thank you.

(A moment of silent empathy, and then JOANNA turns, and EXITS. STEWART stands stage center with the red nose, feeling newly empowered, as the lights dim.)

THE END

LOUIE'S
DAUGHTER

LOUIE'S DAUGHTER was produced by The Theatre Artists Workshop of Westport in Norwalk CT, in October 2003, as part of their annual Playwrights One-Act Festival. It was directed by Frederick Stroppel, and had the following cast:

                A.G..Ken Parker
                WOODY..James Noble
                DONNA...Stacey Nelkin

LOUIE'S DAUGHTER was part of an evening of one-acts titled DANGER, PEOPLE AT LARGE, at the Quick Center for the Arts at Fairfield University in Fairfield, CT, in April 2005. It was produced by Tom Zingarelli and directed by Doug Moser with the following cast and production staff:

                A.G ....Rich Pagnani
                WOODY..James Noble
                DONNA...Joanna Keylock

        Set Designer: Mark Cheney
        Lighting Designer: Nicole Dessin
        Sound Designer: Chris Swetcky
        Soundboard Operator: Joe Boerst
        Lightboard Operator: Zina Skachinksy
        Technical Director: Russ Nagy
        Stage Manager: Theresa Stark

(A corner bar. WOODY, in his mid-70's, wearing a cardigan over a flannel shirt, sits at a table reading the newspaper. He turns the pages with thoughtful deliberation as he leans way forward to pick up every word. The front door opens, and A.G., around 70, wearing a suit and tie, enters and stands at the door.)

A.G.. Whoo-hoo! Have no fear, A.G. is here!

(WOODY doesn't respond, keeps reading the paper. A.G. saunters in, spinning his keys on his finger.)

A.G.. Boy, this place is hopping. Maybe I should have made a reservation. It's not like the old days. *(Sings.)* "Those were the days, my friend, we thought they'd never end..." *(Heads over to the table.)* What's up there, Woodrow?

WOODY. Same shit, different day. Mets lost again. Goddamn mayor is raising the taxes. *(Looks up at A.G.)* What are you all dressed up for?

A.G.. I'm waiting for you to die.

WOODY. *(Goes back to his paper.)* Ha. Won't be long now.

A.G..What, something bothering you?

WOODY. Ahh, I got this thing.

A.G..What thing?

WOODY. Down below. My plumbing.

A.G.. Does it burn?

WOODY. No, just doesn't feel right. You know, coming out in drips and drabs.

A.G.. Maybe it's a little rusty. You can't let the water sit in the pipes.

WOODY. And I'm getting the gout in my knee again. *(Flexes his fingers.)* Not to mention this arthritis. Used to be just when it rained; now it's all the time. And my food doesn't taste so good. Did you ever get that? I'm thinking it's a tumor.

A.G.. You should go to the doctor.

WOODY. *(Shakes his head.)* I only go to the doctor when I feel sick. Otherwise they find something wrong with you. Then you're in the hospital and they're shoving tubes into you, giving you green jell-o... No thanks.

A.G.. That's foolish, Woody. Gotta get your regular check-up. I went to the doctor yesterday, clean bill of health. Took my blood pressure, stuck his finger up my ass, and now I feel great. *(Combs his hair in the bar mirror.)* And I look great. Ready for action. Whoo-hoo! Now if I could just get a drink... *(Yells.)* Hey, Louie! You jerking off back there? *(Shakes head as he sits down next to WOODY.)* No wonder business stinks. He really oughta sell this place. He's lost the drive to succeed. *(Beat.)* So what's going on in the news? Anything I should know about?

WOODY. They found that guy.

A.G.. What guy?

WOODY. From Locust Valley, who disappeared? The lawyer? They thought he was dead?

A.G.. Yeah, they found him? How is he?

WOODY. He's dead.

A.G.. Oh. That's a shame.

WOODY. Yup - murder.

A.G.. *(Skeptical.)* Murder? Come on, that's bullshit.

WOODY. Got whacked or something.

A.G.. Nobody ever gets murdered in this town. In all my years...

WOODY. Says right here.

A.G.. They're just trying to sell their papers. Every time a dead body turns up, they're looking to blame somebody. But what kind of proof do they have - you know what I'm saying? Do they have any real genuine proof?

WOODY. He had a couple of bullet holes in him.

A.G.. Okay, well - question answered.

WOODY. And his head was crushed, so there's reason for suspicion. *(Reads.)* "The body was discovered in a cul de sac off Old Tappen Road."

A.G.. What is that? A cul de sac?

WOODY. I think it's one of those burlap bags, like they put potatoes in.

A.G.. I saw a movie like that once. Guy accidentally opens this trap door over his head, and he gets buried under a whole mound of potatoes. Tough way to go. So "cul" is French for "potato", is that right?

WOODY. *(Disgusted.)* Don't get me started on the French. We saved their asses in World War II, and now when it comes to Iraq, it's fuck you

America. Back-stabbing cocksuckers.

A.G.. All they care about is wine and pastry. That's their big thing.

WOODY. They'll be singing a different tune when the Germans come back. Because one thing's for sure: the Germans always come back.

A.G.. They're very efficient. *(Beat.)* So you like my suit, huh? Evan-Picone.

WOODY. You hit the number or something?

A.G.. I got an interview over at Konica. 1 o'clock.

WOODY. An interview? For what?

A.G.. They're looking for a security guard. Patsy Morano put me on to it.

WOODY. I thought you retired.

A.G.. I got too much energy to sit on my ass all day reading the paper. You gotta stay active, Woody. That's the secret. That's what keeps you going,

WOODY. Ahh. We're getting old, we're gonna die soon - that's the secret.

A.G.. Not me. A.G.'s not goin' nowhere. What's that song? *(Sings "Fame")* "I'm gonna live forever..."

(He dances a bit, and gets a little dizzy. He sits back down to recover).

WOODY. *(Shows A.G. the paper.)* See that tornado in Oklahoma? Wiped out the whole town. Look, there's nothing left standing but the chimney.

A.G.. Why is that a story?

WOODY. People got killed.

A.G.. Yeah, but - Tornadoes in Oklahoma - this is something new? I could have told them that was gonna happen. See, which is why I don't read the paper. Because nothing's new under the sun. A.G. has seen it all.

(DONNA the barmaid enters, and sets down a case of beer.)

DONNA. *(Cheerfully.)* Be right with you!

(DONNA EXITS.)

A.G.. *(Startled.)* What the hell was that?

WOODY. What was what?

A.G.. Was that a barmaid? Did I just see a barmaid, in here?

WOODY. Yeah, that's Donna. She's Louie's daughter.

A.G.. Louie has a daughter? That's a scary fucking thought. Hey, but she's kinda cute, for all that, huh? *(WOODY looks at him.)* What, you don't think so? You're telling me you didn't notice those big brown eyes and the dimples and those nice little titties?

WOODY. You saw all that in what, two seconds?

A.G.. I got a discriminating eye. Is she single?

WOODY. What do you care? *(A.G. smiles.)* Are you for real? She's Louie's daughter.

A.G.. So?

WOODY. So she's got all of Louie's genetical make-up. And sooner or later that shit is gonna seep through.

A.G.. I'm very broadminded when it comes to getting laid.

WOODY. Didn't anybody ever tell you, you're an old goat, you got no business chasing young girls?

A.G.. I don't have to chase them. They come to me. *(Points to his crotch.)* 'Cause A.G.'s still got it where it counts.

WOODY. You must need a crutch for that thing by now.

A.G.. No, siree. I take my Viagra, bada-bing bada-boom, I'm off to the races. *(Pumps his fist.)* Whoo-hoo! Motel time!

WOODY. You're on that stuff? Isabelle must be happy.

A.G.. Isabelle...! I could have a two-day hard-on, she wouldn't give a shit. She's all into "feng shuey" now. Everytime I go home the furniture is all fucked up. So what about you? You want to order some magic pills? Cause if I bring in a new customer, I get free samples.

WOODY. *(Not interested.)* I'm not married anymore, what do I care?

A.G.. Lots of hungry women out there. Why shouldn't you get a little taste?

(DONNA returns with another case of beer. As she bends to put it down, A.G. elbows WOODY.)

A.G.. *(Gesturing at DONNA.)* Hey! Huh? Yeah?

(WOODY shakes his head in disapproval, and turns away to read his paper. A.G. moves over to get closer to DONNA as she straightens up and steps behind the bar.)

DONNA. Hi.

A.G.. *(Puts on the charm.)* Hello, Cinderella.

DONNA. Sorry about that. The night bartender didn't restock, so now it's my job.

A.G.. That's not right.

DONNA. Yeah, kinda pisses me off. The way people take advantage.

A.G.. So you're helping out your old man, huh?

DONNA. Yeah, he had to go over to the liquor board, renew his license.

A.G.. That's great. Gotta carry on the family tradition.

DONNA. Tradition, my ass. I can use the extra cash, that's all. If it were up to me, I'd sell this place tomorrow. My father's a dreamer, he seems to think business is gonna explode any day now.

A.G.. You can't give up hope. That's my motto. *(Extends his hand.)* Allow me to intrude myself: Al Grucci. Everybody calls me A.G.

DONNA. A.G.? What does that stand for?

A.G.. Al Grucci.

DONNA. Oh. Like, duh.

A.G.. And that grouchy old hump over there is Woody.

DONNA. We met. He's very sweet.

A.G.. Oh yeah, he's a peach. *(Whispers.)* You know why they call him Woody, don't you? He's got a wood pecker.

DONNA. He does not!

A.G.. Honest to God. From the war. Check out his palms - they're full of splinters. He has to go to the exterminator every month to get sprayed for termites.

DONNA. You're a big liar.

A.G.. You don't believe me? *(TO WOODY.)* Woody. Come here, we want you to show us something.

WOODY. *(Deep in the paper.)* I'm doing the Jumble.

A.G.. *(To DONNA.)* He's shy. Not like me. I'm very outgoing. In more ways than one, ya know what I'm saying? *(DONNA looks at him blankly.)* How about a little C.C. and soda, honey?

DONNA. C.C.?

A.G.. Canadien Club.

DONNA. Oh. I'm not really good at initials.

A.G.. Don't you worry about it, sweetheart. We all have our talents. *(As DONNA fixes the drink, A.G. looks back over at WOODY. He sticks out his tongue in lascivious glee. WOODY shakes his head, goes back to his paper.)* So how come we haven't seen you around, Cinderella? You on your college break or something?

DONNA. I never went to college.

A.G.. No? Hey, neither did I. That's not important, as long as you have the natural smarts. You got a boyfriend? You gotta have a boyfriend.

DONNA. No boyfriend.

A.G.. Well, I don't believe that. Pretty girl like you? The men have to be awful stupid, is all I have to say. If I were a young man, if I were in the market, let me tell you right now...

DONNA. *(hands him his drink.)* Here you go.

A.G.. Thank you, Beautiful. You don't mind if I call you beautiful, right? Because you are. Anybody ever tell you that?

DONNA. *(Smiles.)* I have to finish stocking up.

A.G.. You go right ahead, honey. A.G.'s not going nowhere.

(DONNA heads into the back. A.G. joins WOODY at the table.)

A.G.. *(Sits down.)* Well, she's got Louie's brains, that's for sure. But with that body, who cares, am I right, huh? That's my kind of woman, no doubt about it. Whoo-hoo!

WOODY. Louie ever catches you fooling around with her, he'll cut your nuts off. See what that does to your Whoo-hoo.

A.G.. There's a law now, says I can't talk to a pretty girl? You gotta loosen up a little, Woody. Have some fun before you die.

WOODY. I have my fun.

A.G.. Yeah, combing the obituaries, what a blast. When's the last time you actually did something?

WOODY. I do things. I take about twenty leaks a day, that's something.

A.G.. We should play a round of golf one of these days. That's good exercise for you.

WOODY. I can't swing a club. My shoulder. *(Lifts his arm halfway up.)* See? That's it.

A.G.. How about, I get back from my interview, we take a ride out to Captree, catch some blues?

WOODY. The blues aren't running yet.

A.G.. All right, fluke, then. Whatever. Just to put some fresh air in your lungs.

WOODY. Too much trouble.

A.G.. What trouble? I'll drive. I'll bait your fucking hook for you.

WOODY. Yeah, but getting on the boat, getting off the boat...

A.G.. Christ, Woody, you gotta make some kind of effort with your life.

WOODY. Fifty years I broke my ass, making an effort. Not anymore. I'm done.

A.G.. You can still have lunch, can't ya? Manny's Clam Bar, we'll get some steamers.

WOODY. All the way to Freeport to eat? I can get a sangwich next door.

A.G.. Jesus, why do you even bother to get out of bed in the morning?

WOODY. Look, I'm happy doin' what I'm doin'. I don't need any goddamn fireworks to make my day.

(DONNA brings in another case of beer, lets it down with a grunt.)

A.G.. *(Watching her with interest.)* Sweet Jesus of Nazareth....

WOODY. *(Reads the paper.)* So it says here, there's some kind of new fish, crawls right out of the water and eats people...

A.G.. *(Rises from his chair.)* Can I help you with something there, Cinderella?

DONNA. No, that's the last of it.

A.G.. You're one strong lady. I'll bet you work out.

DONNA. I like to keep in shape.

A.G.. Look at the size of those arms. Madonna! *(Regards her upper arm.)* What's that tattoo there? Some kind of iguana, yes?

DONNA. It's a Komodo dragon.

A.G.. Right - same thing, practically.

DONNA. I got that in San Francisco. They were running a special.

A.G.. Great town. *(Sings.)* "I left my heart in San Francisco..."

DONNA. I got all kinds of tattoos. I got one here, one there...All over.

A.G.. Maybe someday you'll give me the grand tour, huh?

DONNA. *(A sly smile.)* You're very fresh, you know that?

A.G.. Not fresh. Just well-preserved.

WOODY. *(Shakes his head in disbelief, as he rises from his chair.)* Jesus...!

A.G.. What'd you say, Woodrow?

WOODY. *(Heads to the bathroom.)* I'm gonna go tap a kidney.

A.G.. Go for me, too, while you're in there.

(WOODY EXITS.)

DONNA. How does he do that?

A.G.. Do what?

DONNA. Pee? You know, with a wooden pecker?

A.G.. Gee, I never asked. Some things are private, you know?

DONNA. You would think it would get all warped.

A.G.. *(Smiles.)* Yeah, well, nothing wrong with that. A little dog-leg to the left...Whoo-hoo!

DONNA. You're terrible.

A.G.. You'd better believe it, honey. So what time you get off,? It's Italian Night at the Moose Club. Ziti, sausage and peppers, lots of dancing. They have a live band - Felix Sangenito and his Neapolitan Nifties. Man, they get wailing, they can play all night.

DONNA. Sounds great. *(Points out his wedding ring.)* You should take your wife.

A.G.. She's got osteoporosis. She can't afford to fall down.

DONNA. I'm not a big dancer.

A.G.. I can teach you. A.G. knows all the moves. You do the tarantella? Da-da-da-da, da-da-da, Da-da- da-da da-da-la-da... *(He does a brief tarantella.)* Come on, you'll have fun.

DONNA. Maybe.

A.G.. Maybe? Maybe no, maybe yes?

DONNA. Maybe maybe.

A.G.. Oh, you're teasing. It's not fair to tease an old man.

DONNA. You're not that old.

A.G.. So what do you say then, huh? What do you say? You don't want me going by myself. You get off at six? - I'll pick you up.

DONNA. Seven.

A.G.. Even better. We can go right to the Moose. Get a good parking space.

DONNA. I don't know...

A.G.. What, you got something better to do? Huh?

DONNA. *(After a thought.)* No.

A.G.. You got no boyfriend, right?

DONNA. Right.

(Beat.)

A.G.. So why is that? Pretty girl like you. You don't like men?

DONNA. Let's just say, I've had my experiences. My last boyfriend was a real piece of shit, you'll excuse the expression.

A.G.. It takes all kinds.

DONNA. He was nice in certain ways, don't get me wrong, but there was a lack of basic consideration that I just couldn't get past. When somebody uses your credit card to pay for a hooker, you know? And then I show him the bill, and he says it was just a massage. Like I'm stupid or something, I don't know what a massage costs. And I was supposed to marry this guy. So after that I said, you know, fuck it. I can do without.

A.G.. Sure, you don't need that.

DONNA. I mean, there are women out there who have to take what they can get. But not me. I'm on a different level. I mean, don't you think?

A.G.. Oh, absolutely.

DONNA. I should be able to pick and choose. There's something wrong with the system somewhere.

A.G.. Listen, don't you worry, I'll show you a good time, and I won't expect anything in return. A.G. is a gentleman, head to toe. You see anybody else in this place wearing a suit?

DONNA. I have a lot to offer. I have a lot of depth. Men are so stupid.

A.G.. So, seven o'clock, are we on?

(The PHONE behind the bar rings. DONNA answers it.)

DONNA. *(Into the phone.)* Louie's - can I help you?

(WOODY returns from the bathroom. A.G. joins him at the table.)

A.G.. Any luck?

WOODY. A couple of squirts. Couldn't water a fucking geranium. How about you? *(A.G gives a thumbs-up, to his disbelief.)* No...!

A.G.. A.G.'s getting his Johnson waxed tonight.

WOODY. She said she'd go out with you?

A.G.. She didn't say no. Whoo-hoo! *(WOODY shakes his head.)* What?

WOODY. It's embarrassing.

A.G.. What's embarrassing? That I still got some sensation left in my balls?

WOODY. That you think you got a Chinaman's chance in hell with her.

A.G.. I got myself a date, didn't I? I'll tell you what's embarrassing - these old farts who retire and just roll over and give up. Waiting for the Grim Weeper to take them away.

WOODY. I may be an old fart, but I still have the common sense I was born with. And I know that when you start bird-dogging women half your age, all you're gonna wind up with is an empty wallet and your dick in your hand, and your wife breaking your balls from now till kingdom come. That's a given.

A.G.. Nobody breaks A.G.'s balls. Hey, she's been grabbing my paycheck all these years. now she's getting my pension, she's got a house, a new car last year - I take very good care of her. What A.G. does in his spare time, that's his business.

WOODY. It's all gonna come crashing down on your head like a cul de sac, you'll see. I feel sorry for you.

A.G.. No, I feel sorry for you. Because you got no Life Force working for you. You're all death, death, death. A fucking crepe-hanger. Who croaked today, who's in the hospital, who got hit by a fucking tornado...I don't want to hear it anymore. There's no room in my head for dismal information.

WOODY. I'm just giving you the truth, A.G. You ain't a kid anymore, I don't care how many pills you take.

A.G.. *(Afraid DONNA will overhear.)* Shhh-ush with that.

(But DONNA has a finger in her ear as she talks on the phone.)

WOODY. *(Scoffs.)* She's talking to her boyfriend, she ain't listening to us. .

A.G.. She doesn't have a boyfriend - shows what you know. She's holding out for something better.

WOODY. What, like you? She's been waiting for you all her life? You're the answer to every girl's prayers, aren't you? Ha!

A.G.. You know - I got a big interview coming up, I gotta put myself in a positive frame of mind. I can't be imbibing this shit.

WOODY. You'll see.

A.G.. No, you'll see. You'll be sitting in this same fucking chair till the day you die, reading the same fucking paper cover to cover, while I'm out there living, and having a life.

WOODY. And making a big fucking fool of yourself. Have fun.

A.G.. I will have fun. I'll have more fun than you ever dreamed of.

WOODY. You're still gonna die, my friend. Ain't no pills for that. *(Reading the paper.)* You're still gonna die...

A.G.. You think you know everything, don't you? Don't you?

(A.G. grabs the newspaper away from WOODY.)

WOODY. Hey!

A.G.. How much you know now, huh? Huh?

WOODY. Give me that.

A.G.. Not so big, without your precious Newsday to back you up, are you?

WOODY. I'm still reading that. Quit fucking around.

A.G.. I'm a fool? What about you? - *(In a baby voice.)* "My paper, give me my paper, I want my paper...!"

WOODY. Goddamn it, I'm not kidding!

A.G.. You want it? You want it? Okay - Whoo-hoo! *(A.G. tosses the newspaper into the air, and the pages scatter to the floor.)* There! That's what I think of you and all your shitty advice.

WOODY. What the hell is wrong with you? Pick that up.

A.G.. You pick it up. Be nice to see you get off your ass and do something for a change.

WOODY. I'm not picking it up. You pick it up! *(A.G. shrugs, doesn't move.)* You're a goddamn idiot. I paid good money for that paper.

(A.G. reaches into his pocket and throws some coins at WOODY.)

A.G.. Here. A.G.'s not cheap.

WOODY. *(Rising, insulted by the gesture.)* You want to take this outside?

A.G.. Are you calling me out?

WOODY. Are you calling me out? That's the question.

A.G.. *(Dismissive.)* Come on, Woody. You're in no condition, with your fucking gout.

WOODY. I can still kick your guinea ass.

A.G.. That'll be the day.

WOODY. No, this'll be the day.

A.G.. Yeah?

WOODY. Yeah!

A.G.. Yeah?

(They glare at each other. DONNA is just hanging up the phone.)

DONNA. What are you guys doing?
WOODY. Nothing.
A.G.. We're having a difference of opinion.
DONNA. You oughta calm down. You're gonna both have heart attacks.

(WOODY sits back down.)

A.G.. *(Buttoning his jacket.)* Well...I got my interview. *(To DONNA.)* So, Cinderella, I'll see you at seven?
DONNA. Oh, tonight? I don't think so.
A.G.. What?
DONNA. No, that was my girlfriend on the phone. She's in town from Boston, and this is her only night, so we're gonna hang.
A.G.. She can come along. The more the merrier.
DONNA. No, I don't think she'd be into it. Italian music and all that.
A.G.. It's not all Italian. They do big band, too.
DONNA. She just wants to chill, so...
A.G.. *(Getting it.)* Oh.
DONNA. Sorry.
A.G.. Hey, A.G. doesn't need anybody to have a good time. That's nice, that you stick by your friend. That's very admirable.
DONNA. Maybe some other time.
A.G.. A.G.'s a busy man, but we'll see.
DONNA. Yeah. I gotta get some ice for the bins here.

(DONNA EXITS with an ice bucket. A.G. and WOODY exchange a look.)

A.G.. Fuck her, anyway. She's no prize.
WOODY. Plenty of fish in the sea, A.G.
A.G.. You got that right. You see all those fucking tattoos she's got? Louie's daughter.
WOODY. Exactly what I was saying.
A.G.. I like classy women. "Maybe some other time...", she says. Don't hold your breath, honey. He travels fastest who travels by himself, you know what I'm saying?.
WOODY. Some things aren't meant to be.

(Beat.)

A.G.. You sure you don't want to go to lunch?
WOODY. Pick up my paper first, then we'll talk about lunch.

(A.G. takes a step towards the papers, and then changes his mind.)

A.G.. Who wants to eat with you, anyway, you crabby old fuck? *(Takes out his keys.)* A.G.'s leaving the building.
WOODY. Hey, my paper -!
A.G.. *(Heading out the door.)* Whoo-hoo!
WOODY. - son-of-a-bitch —!

(But A.G. is gone. WOODY sighs, lifts himself out of the chair, and starts gathering up the newspaper. DONNA returns with a bucket full of ice.)

DONNA. *(Looking around.)* Is he gone?
WOODY. He's gone. *(Straightening up.)* That was really your girl-friend on the phone?
DONNA. Yeah - but she's not here, she's still in Boston. I was just trying to be nice. That's what I hate about this business: you have to be nice to everyone, regardless.
WOODY. He likes to throw the bull around, but he's harmless.
DONNA. He thinks he's some kind of great lover, Casanova or some-thing. Doesn't he know how old he is? Don't get me wrong - I've gone out with lots of old guys before, and some of them were very interesting. But, you know - the Moose Club! Jesus Christ! Maybe in fifty years.
WOODY. They always put out a good spread.
DONNA. I deserve better - that's all I have to say. *(Beat.)* So is that true, what he said?
WOODY. What did he say?
DONNA. You have a wooden...you know?
WOODY. What? A wooden leg? No, that's just my gout. Acts up once in a while. I still got both legs I was born with.
DONNA. No, he said... Never mind. I'm just stupid, that's all. *(Beat.)* When does it start getting busy around here?
WOODY. Oh, in a couple of hours. Maybe. *(Reading the paper.)* So they found that lawyer. The guy from Locust Valley, who disappeared?

He was in a potato sack.

(He turns the page.)

DONNA. God, we oughta sell this place.

(Lights fade)

GLACIER BAY

GLACIER BAY was produced by The Theatre Artists Workshop of Westport in Norwalk Ct., in October 2003, as part of their annual Playwrights One-Act Festival. It was directed by Chilton Ryan, and had the following cast:

ARTIE..James Noble
CONNIE..Brett Somers
JILL..Katie Sparer

GLACIER BAY was part of an evening of one-acts titled DANGER, PEOPLE AT LARGE, at the Quick Center for the Arts at Fairfield University in Fairfield, CT, in April 2005. It was produced by Tom Zingarelli and directed by Doug Moser with the following cast and production staff:

ARTIE..Jack Klugman
CONNIE......................................Brett Somers
JILL..Joanna Keylock

Set Designer: Mark Cheney
Lighting Designer: Nicole Dessin
Sound Designer: Chris Swetcky
Soundboard Operator: Joe Boerst
Lightboard Operator: Zina Skachinksy
Technical Director: Russ Nagy
Stage Manager: Theresa Stark

(A SIDE ROOM at a RECEPTION HALL. ARTIE, in his mid-70's, ENTERS, holding a plate filled with appetizers in one hand, and a drink in the other. He makes an awkward attempt to eat with his hands full, and winds up dropping an appetizer on the floor.)

ARTIE. Ahhh...Shit.

(He thinks about bending over to pick it up, and then decides to kick it out of the way. He kicks repeatedly at it, not really moving it very far. CONNIE, 70ish, enters with a plate and a drink.)

CONNIE. Did you get any crabcakes? There was a boy bringing around little crabcakes. What are you doing?
ARTIE. I dropped a shrimp on the floor.
CONNIE. Well, leave it there. Here's a table. Let's grab it before somebody else gets it. *(As ARTIE still kicks at it.)* Artie! Leave it. They have people for that.
ARTIE. *(As he goes to the table.)* Somebody could trip over it.
CONNIE. *(Sitting down.)* It's a shrimp. Who's gonna trip over it? Some midget?
ARTIE. *(Looks around.)* There's a midget? Where?
CONNIE. Here, sit down. *(Sharply.)* Artie!

(ARTIE puts his plate and drink on the table. But instead of sitting, he heads back over to pick up the appetizer.)

CONNIE. What are you doing? Leave it.
ARTIE. I just want to get it off the floor...
CONNIE. Leave it, Leave it!
ARTIE. I will. *(Bending to get the shrimp.)* I just want to pick it up, that's all...

(He grunts as he creakily tries to pick up the shrimp.)

CONNIE. *(Sighs.)* Okay, fine - fall right on your head. Won't do you any harm, that's for sure.

(ARTIE bends lower and lower, and finally picks up the shrimp.)

ARTIE. Gotcha! *(He drops the shrimp again.)* Aagh! *(Bends with a grunt.)* It's wrapped in bacon, very slippery... *(He finally snares the shrimp.)* Ah! *(And he slowly straightens up.)*

CONNIE. Now what are you going to do with it?

ARTIE. *(Casts about.)* Should be a trash can, something...?

CONNIE. *(Holds out a napkin.)* Here. I have a napkin.

ARTIE. *(Mis-hearing.)* What? You want a napkin?

(ARTIE starts out.)

CONNIE. No, I have one right here!

ARTIE. It's not a problem, I have to throw this out anyway...

CONNIE. *(Sharply.)* Artie! Put-the-shrimp-in-the-napkin!

ARTIE. *(Finally understands.)* Oh. I can just put the shrimp in the napkin. *(ARTIE shuffles over and puts the shrimp in the napkin.)* There. Just as simple as that.

CONNIE. *(Shakes her head.)* God Almighty, the smallest little thing and it's like scaling Everest.

ARTIE. *(Sits down.)* Ahhh! Now we're all set. This is the best food, at the cocktail hour.

CONNIE. You have too much fried stuff on your plate. Your cholesterol.

ARTIE. Oh, my cholesterol, my ass. We never had cholesterol in the old days. If you ever told my father that he had cholesterol, he'd tell you to go shit in your hat.

CONNIE. Nice talk.

ARTIE. That's what he'd say. That was his favorite expression. "Dad, can I borrow the car?" - "Go shit in your hat." "Dad, can you sign my report card?" - "Go shit in your hat." *(Chuckles.)* He was a funny man.

CONNIE. Here comes Jill. Watch what you say.

ARTIE. Who's Jill?

(JILL ENTERS.)

JILL. Aunt Connie! Uncle Artie!
CONNIE. *(Brightly.)* Hello, Jill!

(ARTIE starts to get up.)

JILL. No, don't get up.
CONNIE. *(Holds ARTIE down.)* Don't get up. *(To JILL.)* What a lovely affair. This is a lovely, lovely place.
JILL. I'm so glad you could make it.
CONNIE. Oh, we wouldn't have missed it for the world. Would we, Artie?
ARTIE. Who brought the midget?
JILL. *(Passes over this.)* It means a lot to Michael that you could both be here for his big day.
CONNIE. Little Michael...! He's gotten so tall. Shot up like a beanpole.
ARTIE. He looks just like his father. *(CONNIE gasps, and kicks at him under the table.)* Ahh! What?
JILL. Anyway, it's so good to see you. Family is so important, especially nowadays.
CONNIE. Oh, absolutely.
JILL. Now that Mom and Dad are gone, you two are all I have left...

(JILL starts to cry.)

CONNIE. Well, we're not going anywhere soon. *(Glances at ARTIE.)* At least I'm not.
JILL. *(Wiping her tears.)* I'm sorry. This is supposed to be a happy day. I have to check on the catering staff, make sure they're not goofing off... *(Brightly.)* But we'll catch up later, and we'll talk.
CONNIE. That'll be nice.

(JILL EXITS.)

CONNIE. *(Contemptuous.)* Her and her fake tears. Always has to put on a show. Two-faced phony.
ARTIE. Say, what did you kick me for? That hurt!
CONNIE. "He looks like his father..."! You don't even know his father.

ARTIE. I was just being polite.

CONNIE. His father was black.

ARTIE. So, he was black. These things happen.

CONNIE. So, Michael has light skin; he doesn't look black at all.

ARTIE. All right, he looks like his stepfather, then. What's the difference? You don't have to attack me. *(Rubs his leg.)* Got me right on the anklebone, goddammit...

CONNIE. You're a constant embarrassment, it never ends.

ARTIE. Now I'll have a bone bruise. I hope you're happy. *(Looks at her plate.)* Where are the crabcakes? You ate them already?

CONNIE. I didn't get any crabcakes.

ARTIE. I thought you said...

CONNIE. I said there were crabcakes going around. I didn't get any, I don't like crabcakes.

ARTIE. But I like them.

CONNIE. I know you do. That's why I said, you missed them.

ARTIE. Oh, I get it. Fuck me, in other words.

CONNIE. That's not necessary.

ARTIE. God forbid you give me a second thought.

CONNIE. They'll come around again.

ARTIE. Don't try to placate me. You know what happens, these cocktail hours, they just keep bringing out trays of potato puffs and zucchini things, all the cheap crap, and then once in a blue moon, crabcakes. We'll never see them again.

CONNIE. You've got enough on your plate already.

ARTIE. I want crabcakes!

CONNIE. *(Sharply.)* Artie...!

(ARTIE is silenced. Beat, as they eat.)

ARTIE. What is this whole shebang for, anyway?

CONNIE. It's for Michael.

ARTIE. I know, but for what? Is it an engagement party?

CONNIE. An engagement party? The kid's barely thirteen.

ARTIE. Well, I don't know. Did he graduate or something?

CONNIE. Graduate from what? He's Jill's son; he's lucky he can spell.

ARTIE. So what's it for, then - you're so smart?

CONNIE. It's for...It's for...

ARTIE. See, you don't know either.

SENIOR MOMENTS

CONNIE. I do know. It's for... *(Can't remember.)* Shit!

ARTIE. Ha ha!

CONNIE. I know the word. It's on the tip of my tongue... Oh, I know - it's his Circumcision!

ARTIE. *(Laughs.)* His what?

CONNIE. *(Shakes her head.)* I mean... his Confirmation.

ARTIE. *(Still laughing.)* He just got circumsized? No wonder he's so white.

CONNIE. His Confirmation. I got the words mixed up.

ARTIE. You're getting as bad as me.

CONNIE. Nobody's as bad as you.

ARTIE. This is how it starts. I remember when I started forgetting. It's the beginning of the end.

CONNIE. Oh, clam up, you old coot. The day I get like you, you can take me out and shoot me.

ARTIE. It'll be my pleasure. So if it's his Confirmation, how come we didn't go to the church?

CONNIE. We did go to the church. We were just at the church.

ARTIE. I didn't go to any church. I don't know what you're talking about.

CONNIE. See, don't ever compare me to you. I may be a little forgetful, but you're missing half your brain. The good half.

ARTIE. What church was it?

CONNIE. St. Dominic's.

ARTIE. *(Scoffs.)* St. Dominic's? I haven't been to St. Dominic's in, I don't know how long. Since I was a kid.

CONNIE. *(Pulls the church bulletin from her bag.)* Look, here's the church bulletin. For God's sake, it was just an hour ago, and you can't remember. I'll bet you can't even tell me what you just put in your mouth. Can you?

ARTIE. It was... *(Thinks.)*

CONNIE. Come on, come on.

ARTIE. Well, it wasn't crabcakes, I know that.

CONNIE. It was a mozzarella stick. Fried garbage. And shrimp with bacon. All cholesterol. Might as well just shove Crisco oil up your arteries.

ARTIE. Who cares, at my age? I'm gonna lose, what, ten minutes off my life?

CONNIE. And bacon is full of carcinogens, too. Cancer - that's no joke.

ARTIE. Let me ask you this: did you ever see a pig with cancer? Ever?

CONNIE. Where am I going to see a pig? Who am I, Ma Kettle?

ARTIE. You said it, not me.

.   CONNIE. Besides, pigs never have a chance to get cancer - they all get slaughtered first.

ARTIE. Oh, you have an answer for everything. We should all be as brilliant as you!

CONNIE. *(Points to her wedding ring.)* If I were so brilliant I wouldn't be wearing this damn thing. I'd be free and clear. My age, and I'm still babysitting. There's no justice... *(Suddenly notices.)* And where's your wedding ring?

ARTIE. My...?

CONNIE. For Christ's sake, you lost it again?

ARTIE. (Looks at his finger.) I'll be a goddamned son-of-a-bitch.

CONNIE. I told you not to take it off.

ARTIE. I didn't - it musta fell off.

(ARTIE looks on the floor.)

CONNIE. Fell off! I'm supposed to believe that?

ARTIE. Because my fingers are shrinking. Look. *(Holds his hand up, fingers spread.)* You can see right through them.

CONNIE. When you were talking to that woman - that's when you lost it. I know.

ARTIE. What woman?

CONNIE. The woman in the lobby, with the brown hair and the big bazooms. I saw you.

ARTIE. Brown hair?

CONNIE. Talking about something, very chatty, and she was touching your arm. What was that all about, I'd like to know? And you just lose your wedding ring, "coincidentally"...!

ARTIE. Hey, if some strange woman wants to touch my arm, what can I do about it? Charisma is its own reward.

CONNIE. Lecherous old fool. As if there were the remotest possibility...!

ARTIE. What? You think I couldn't handle a little something on the side? *(Points to his hair.)* Just because there's snow on the oven... And don't talk about me - what about you?

CONNIE. What about me?

SENIOR MOMENTS

ARTIE. I'm no stooge - I saw you kissing that plumber. Think you can put one over on me...?

CONNIE. What plumber?

ARTIE. That plumber. That...Tom Gilroy. I saw you. Over there by the potted plant. You kissed him.

CONNIE. Tom Guilfoy. And he's not a plumber anymore. He has his own contracting business. He could buy and sell us a dozen times over.

ARTIE. Smelly bastard used to clean our pipes. Hoping to return the favor, are you?

CONNIE. Stop that disgusting talk. You think you're being funny? You're being disgusting.

ARTIE. You kissed him, that's all I know.

CONNIE. It's a party. You have to kiss everybody.

ARTIE. I'll bet you didn't kiss that midget.

CONNIE. There's no midget!

ARTIE. Sure, that's what you say now. For all I know he could be stashed under the table.

CONNIE. *(Shakes her head.)* When, God? - When are you going to put an end to this?

ARTIE. I'm no stooge. You have to get up pretty early in the morning, Lois...

CONNIE. My name is Connie!

ARTIE. Lois, Connie...All I'm saying is...

CONNIE. *(Abruptly.)* What are you saying? What?

(ARTIE stops, stares blankly, as he tries to remember.)

CONNIE. *(She puts the fork in his hand.)* Here. Eat your crabcakes.

ARTIE. I don't have any -

CONNIE. Well, eat whatever's there!

(Beat.)

CONNIE. *(Muses.)* No justice. All the things we were planning to do when you retired... The golf, the vacation trips. Alaska, remember? The cruise on Glacier Bay, with the whales and the Kodiak bears, we talked about it all the time...Never came to anything. Well, we had our good times, didn't we? Nothing lasts forever. It's not your fault you're sick.

ARTIE. I'm not sick. I'm just slowing down a little, that's all.

CONNIE. You don't even know where you are half the time. You don't know what year it is, you don't know who's alive or who's dead... *(ARTIE reaches down under the table.)* What are you doing?

ARTIE. *(Rubs his ankle.)* My ankle hurts. I must have banged it against something.

CONNIE. It's all a blur, isn't it? Yesterday, fifty years ago, it's all the same. Hard to believe. You used to be such a man, so in control...And a good dresser, too. If you could see the way you look now...! But you were a lot of fun, Artie, I give you that. We had a lot of laughs, when we weren't at each other's throats... *(She and ARTIE share a laugh, and then she grows sad.)* I miss you, Artie. I miss you.

(Beat.)

ARTIE. *(Stirring.)* That's a load of shit. You don't care about me. You never cared about me.

CONNIE. *(Exasperated.)* Oh, Christ. Here we go...

ASRTIE. *(Mockingly.)* "I miss you..." Sure - if it was up to you I'd be in a home by now.

CONNIE. It is up to me. And you should be in a home. I keep putting up with you because I have a good heart.

ARTIE. Because you have a good deal, and you don't want to jump off the gravy train. I know your game - you live off my money, let me work myself into an early grave, and go off and do what you like, you think I don't notice. I saw you kissing that midget. I'm no stooge. And he's not the only one. Ed Kaplicki.

CONNIE. Oh, Jesus...

ARTIE. Ed Kaplicki! There's a prick from the past.

CONNIE. Language...!

ARTIE. You thought you were so smart. The book club. "I'm going to my book club." Going to the Crow's Nest Motel with Ed Kaplicki!

CONNIE. You don't know what you're talking about. You saw that in a movie or something.

ARTIE. You're a fucking whore, you always were.

CONNIE. Artie! Do you want me to stick this fork in your eye? Do you?

ARTIE. Go ahead, put me in a home. Put me in Montclair. Just like you did with your own father.

CONNIE. *(Tersely.)* You just shut up about that.

SENIOR MOMENTS

ARTIE. Poor old fellow, never hurt anybody, and you let him waste away like a pathetic piece of nothing. Never even visited him.

CONNIE. I visited him all the... Just stop it.

ARTIE. I used to go up there - I used to go - see him, his arms were like bones, little sticks, you could put your fingers around them. That's how they treat you in Montclair. You wanna stick me in there? That's fine. Typical. Vindictive ungrateful whore.

CONNIE. I'm telling you to shut up...

ARTIE. If I ever tried to put my father in a home, he'd tell me to go shit in my hat. And he'd be right! You don't do that to your father!

CONNIE. *(Gets up.)* That's it. I've had enough.

ARTIE. Fucking Ed Kaplicki! As if you ever read a book in your life!

CONNIE. You're a sick old man, Artie, and you're gonna die alone, and I feel sorry for you, but I don't need this shit anymore!

ARTIE. Couldn't even get me a fucking crabcake...! Miserable bitch!

CONNIE. That's right, I'm miserable! And who made me that way? You, you useless bloodsucking old fart. I know, I'm supposed to take care of you, stick with you till death do us part. Well, the hell with that! You're on your own! I don't care what you do! Go shit in *your* hat! Okay? Okay?

(JILL returns.)

JILL. *(Brightly.)* We're just about ready to go into the main room. *(In the ensuing silence.)* What's the matter?

CONNIE. Nothing's the matter. Everything's fine. I'm just leaving, that's all. *(To ARTIE.)* And don't try to follow me!

JILL. Are you feeling sick?

CONNIE. Yes, I'm sick - sick of him! I'm sorry, Jill, I know this is a special day for you and your Michael, but I've had it with this idiot. I've just had it.

JILL. What do you mean?

CONNIE. He knows what I mean. A divorce is what I mean. Oh, I know what everybody's going to say, for better or for worse, he's sick in the head, blah blah blah... but I've done my time, I've lost too many years. I have to think of myself for a change. I'm still young, I'm still alive! *(JILL chuckles to herself.)* What are you laughing at? You think it's funny? Not to me. I'm out. Out! Free and clear!

JILL. Now you know you can't divorce Uncle Artie.

CONNIE. Oh, I can't? Just watch me.

ARTIE.Well, maybe I'll divorce you first. Mental cruelty.

CONNIE. You don't have anything mental left, you dopey dillcock. *(To JILL.)* He thinks I'm kidding. I'm not kidding.

JILL. Aunt Connie...

CONNIE. I'll get myself a good Jew lawyer and divorce the shit out of him. *(To ARTIE.)* That's right, I'm taking the gravy with me! We'll see who's the stooge here...!

JILL. Aunt Connie, listen to me, listen...

CONNIE. I'm listening - What?

JILL. *(Gently.)* You're not married anymore.

(Beat.)

CONNIE. What?

JILL. You're not married to Artie anymore. So you can't get divorced.

ARTIE. What did she say?

CONNIE. She said...That's supposed to be a joke? That's not funny, Jill, not funny at all. We're not married...! I wish! *(Points to her wedding ring.)* Look, what do you call this?

JILL. It's your wedding ring.

CONNIE. Of course it is.

JILL. You're married to Tom now.

CONNIE. Tom?

JILL. Tom Guilfoy.

CONNIE. Tom Guilfoy?

JILL. He's your husband. You know that.

CONNIE. Tom Guilfoy?

ARTIE. I knew there was something going on between you.

CONNIE. Why would I marry Tom Guilfoy?

JILL. I don't know, but you did. *(Laughs.)* So you two have been sitting here all this time, and...? *(Catches herself.)* I'm sorry - but it is funny... Do you feel all right?

ARTIE.*(Amused.)* Yep, this is how it starts. I remember when I started forgetting who I was married to...

CONNIE. Oh, shut up, will you? *(To JILL.)* Of course I'm all right. I knew we were divorced all along. I was just having fun.

ARTIE. Sure you were. *(To JILL.)* And she was trying to tell me I was in church. I knew goddamn well I wasn't in any fucking church. *(Brightly.)* So what about me? Who am I hitched to now?

JILL. You're not, Uncle Artie. You're a single man on the loose.

ARTIE. Ah - The bachelor life! That's for me! Bring on the girls, bring 'em on!

CONNIE. *(As she remembers, quietly to JILL.)* He's in Montclair now, isn't he? *(JILL nods.)* So that woman he was with...

JILL. That's his nurse. She's coming back at six. Unless we need her sooner. *(To ARTIE.)* But you're okay, Uncle Artie, aren't you?

ARTIE. Couldn't be better. Ready to take on the world! Ha ha!

JILL. *(Reflects to CONNIE.)* It's so sad. The two of you, you both mean so much to me, and now... *(She wipes away more tears.)* Okay, well... I have to make the toast. Do you need anything? Do you want me to get Tom?

CONNIE. No, I'm fine. I'm fine.

(JILL heads out.)

ARTIE. *(Calls after her.)* If you see any of those crabcakes floating around... *(Beat.)* I remember the time I thought I was married to Dorothy Lamour. Hot damn.

(CONNIE looks in her wallet, checks her license.)

CONNIE. Constance Guilfoy. 18 Kenilworth Drive.

ARTIE. She was in one of those sarongs. Big flower in her ear.

CONNIE. *(Realizing.)* That's where I live. We have a big yellow house, with rhododendrons. Tom.

ARTIE. Sure. We got divorced years ago. I knew that. *(Beat.)* Well, don't worry. It's not like a death sentence, you know. Look at me. You could go on for years and years and years like this - lose a little bit more every day - and I'll tell you something, it doesn't matter a damn, because it's just one less thing you have to think about. Everything gets a little easier, day by day. God knows what He's doing.

CONNIE. *(Reflects.)* I guess it is funny.

ARTIE. Oh, sure. All those Road movies, she made with Hope and Crosby. Laugh your ass off. Good clean fun, too. Not like nowadays. *(Sings.)* "Sweet Leilani, Heavenly flower..."

CONNIE. Come on - it's time to go inside. She's giving the toast. You need help?

ARTIE. *(Scoffs.)* That'll be the day, I need help.

(ARTIE grunts as he tries to get up out of the chair. CONNIE offers her arm, and ARTIE grabs it)

ARTIE. Okay, I've got you.

(They start out.)

ARTIE. *(Limping.)* My goddamn ankle hurts....
CONNIE. Watch your step. It's slippery there.

(CONNIE and ARTIE slowly walk out.)

Other Plays
by
Frederick Stroppel...

A Chance Meeting
Actor!
Chain Mail
The Christmas Spirit
Coelacanth
Crashing the Gate
Designated Driver
Do Over
Domestic Violence
Fortune's Fools
Friendly Fire
A Good Man
Harvest Time
Itch
Judgment Call
Mamet Women
Morning Coffee
One Man's Vision
Package Deal
Perfect Pitch
Single and Proud
Smoke-Out
Soulmates
Tangled Web
Tree World
Twenty Years Ago

Please visit
www.samuelfrench.com
or consult our **Basic Catalogue of Plays and Musicals** *for Complete details*

OTHER TITLES AVAILABLE FROM SAMUEL FRENCH

TAKE HER, SHE'S MINE
Phoebe and Henry Ephron

Comedy / 11m, 6f / Various Sets
Art Carney and Phyllis Thaxter played the Broadway roles of parents of two typical American girls enroute to college. The story is based on the wild and wooly experiences the authors had with their daughters, Nora Ephron and Delia Ephron, themselves now well known writers. The phases of a girl's life are cause for enjoyment except to fearful fathers. Through the first two years, the authors tell us, college girls are frightfully sophisticated about all departments of human life. Then they pass into the "liberal" period of causes and humanitarianism, and some into the intellectual lethargy of beatniksville. Finally, they start to think seriously of their lives as grown ups. It's an experience in growing up, as much for the parents as for the girls.

"A warming comedy. A delightful play about parents vs kids. It's loaded with laughs. It's going to be a smash hit."
– *New York Mirror*